C0-ARE-329

THE WONDERFUL TUMBLE OF
Timothy Smith

THE WONDERFUL TUMBLE

by Doris Faber

Illustrated by Leonard Shortall

NEW YORK: Alfred A. Knopf, *1958*

of TIMOTHY SMITH

L. C. catalog card number: 58–12358

© DORIS FABER, 1958

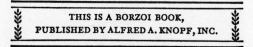

THIS IS A BORZOI BOOK,
PUBLISHED BY ALFRED A. KNOPF, INC.

COPYRIGHT 1958 BY DORIS FABER. All rights reserved. No part of this book may be reproduced in any form without permission in writing from the publisher, except by a reviewer who may quote brief passages and reproduce not more than three illustrations in a review to be printed in a magazine or newspaper. Manufactured in the United States of America. Distributed simultaneously in Canada by Random House of Canada, Limited, Toronto.

CONTENTS

THE WONDERFUL TUMBLE OF
Timothy Smith

Out of the Tree House

YOU wouldn't think the whole town would cheer because Timothy Smith tumbled out of his tree house, would you?

That a real parade would start at the Fire House and toot on past the stores and Purdy's Park . . . to the old railroad station, of all places?

Oompah! Oompah! went the high school band, the players splendid in their crimson suits with the shiny gold stripes that gleamed in the sun.

Little children squealed and wriggled on their fathers' shoulders. The Girl Scouts were

[3]

there, the Boy Scouts were there, just about everybody in town was there.

Then Mayor Tweedy raised his hand for quiet, and . . .

And it all happened because Timothy Smith tumbled out of his tree house on a nice warm morning in August.

Luckily, the grass was soft under the gnarled gray apple branch that his ladder was lashed to. The ladder and the board floor it led up to were perfectly solid—altogether a very good tree house in the old giant apple tree left over from when the Smith's whole yard was part of an orchard.

Maybe it might not have been wise to let all the nearly-nine-year-old boys for blocks around go climbing in that tree. Its old boughs were tough enough, but if the tree did happen to produce a few apples bigger than golf balls, those boys were sure to start munching, and there would go the crop.

"Oh, well," said Mr. Smith. "That is a good

[4]

branch to put a ladder against, right there on the left. And, right above it, not bad at all to run a floor across. Not too high, either."

But if you happened to be watching a bluebird winging down from one of the really high branches—well, anyone can lose his footing and take a tumble.

"Ouch!" Timothy said that sunny August morning, rolling onto his skinny, blue-jeaned bottom and trying to sit up on the grass.

Timothy's sister, Nan, jumped off the swing and came running, her light brown pony tails bouncing furiously. Everybody knows a sister who is almost seven can sometimes make an awful fuss about a brother two years and two days older than she is.

"Did you HURT yourself?" Nan hollered. Her large blue eyes were huge with alarm. "Should I call Mom?"

"What for?" said Timothy, putting a fierce scowl on his sunburned face that was almost the same shade as his short, reddish hair. "It's

[5]

just a little—ouch! Okay, call her. I guess I broke my arm or something."

But it turned out to be a twisted wrist, that's all. Just enough to call off climbing, swimming, and throwing until the end of the week.

Climbing!

Swimming!

Throwing!

What else was a nearly-nine-year-old boy to do in a hot spell in August? Even for just a few days?

"How about berry-picking?" Nan asked when they had flopped onto the porch glider. They had just come home after having his wrist taped. "I'll carry the pot, and you can use your right hand to pick."

Timothy shook his head. Not much fun that way.

"Well," said Nan, "how about making a village on the moon again? In my old sand-box."

[6]

"Say!" Timothy said. Then the eager look faded from his face.

"Nope." He shook his head. "Not enough sand left. Mom used it up when she was filling some flower pots."

But suddenly the eager look flashed back.

"I have it!" said Timothy, making the glider give a tremendous swoop.

"What?" Nan's eyebrows went up to her bangs.

"Telescope!"

"What's a telescope?" said Nan. "I know it's something about looking, but what—"

"It's just exactly what I need for the old tree house," Timothy said. "You look through it, and you can see things closer. The moon and stars and things."

"Oh!" said Nan. "But don't you need something special to make it with? A motor, or something like that?"

Timothy now gave her the withering

[8]

glance that any boy would give a girl who made such a silly statement.

"You don't need a motor," he said, and shook his head. "It's a thing you look through, like eyeglasses. Fancy eyeglasses. Wow! That's right!"

"What's right?" said Nan, too interested to be insulted.

"Eyeglasses, that's what I'll need," Timothy

said thoughtfully. "Dad told me about how a telescope is like an eyeglass glass attached to the top and bottom of a tube and—"

"Like toothpaste?" said Nan. The sly little bounce of her pony tails showed she wasn't really serious.

"Of all the . . ." Then Timothy had to grin. "Not that kind of a tube," he said. "The kind a new calendar comes in. One of those long, round cardboard jobs. Well, if we just take the glass parts out of an old pair of eye-glasses, we can . . ."

So pleased to hear him saying "we," instead of "I," the way he might have on a project such as this, Nan listened extra carefully.

". . . we can attach one piece of glass to the top of the tube and the other to the bottom," he was saying. "But wait a minute!" Timothy wrinkled his sunburned forehead.

"What's the matter?" Nan asked anxiously.

"I don't know if it would work with pieces

from the same pair of eyeglasses," Timothy said. "I sort of think one piece of glass has to be smaller than the other, or something."

He started to chew one corner of his lower lip, and that meant he was deep in thought.

"They don't have some kind of kits in a store for making telescopes, do they?" Nan said. "Maybe we could pick some blackberries, after all, and get enough money to . . ."

Timothy shook his head.

"Well, then," said Nan, "maybe Dad could tell us how tonight."

"Who wants to wait till tonight?" Timothy said.

Nan sighed.

"I don't guess Mom could—" she was saying, when Timothy stood up with a rush that made the glider dance.

"Where're you going?" Nan shouted, trying to stop the rocking so she could hop down, too.

[11]

"Library!" called Timothy over his shoulder. "Got to see if Mom will drive us to the library."

"Ooooooooooh!" said Nan. It made her blue eyes grow just enormous to think of how her brother always could come up with the answer to any problem, for instance, this idea of looking for a book to tell about building telescopes. Timothy was certainly a thinker!

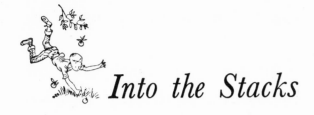 *Into the Stacks*

"OH DEAR! Dear me!" said Miss Wickersham.

Miss Wickersham was the librarian, a plump little gray-haired lady, not much taller than Timothy himself.

"If you were interested in magnets, Timothy, we have a lovely book," she said. "With a whole lot of pictures, too. Of experiments."

Timothy shook his head, just as Nan knew he would.

"We did magnets in the first grade," he said.

"Oh, yes," said Miss Wickersham. "Of

course. I should remember . . ." And she pulled down the corners of her mouth, trying to hide a smile that showed she did remember.

Timothy's mother laughed right out loud, making three or four people bending over books look up quickly. This was an awfully tiny library, just one crowded, shelf-lined room above the garage where all the village trucks were kept. If you didn't whisper, you were bound to disturb somebody.

"Oh!" said Mrs. Smith. "I'm sorry." Then in a properly hushed voice she said: "I still expect to find a magnet in the apple sauce whenever I take a jar out of the refrigerator. Timothy did magnets, no doubt about it."

Timothy let out a little huffing sound you might call a snort. He still did not see what was so funny about testing magnets all around the house, to make sure they would do what the book said they would. Who could help it if the lid had slipped off a jar of apple sauce?

[14]

But that . . . and snakes . . . and scare-crows . . . were all things of the past. The question now was how to build a telescope.

"If you don't have any books on telescopes, could you tell me—" he started.

"It isn't really that we don't have any books on telescopes," Miss Wickersham said kindly. "I'm sure there are three or four down in the stacks in the basement."

"Can we go look?" Timothy asked.

"I'm afraid not," Miss Wickersham said. "The library board is very particular about who goes down. You see, everything is in a sort of order, the way we had it before we had to move out of Town Hall to make room for the police. And if any book gets out of its place"—she spread out her hands and sighed —"I just don't know if we'd ever be able to find it again in that dark old basement."

"But aren't you going to get your new building soon?" Mrs. Smith asked.

Miss Wickersham shook her head sadly.

"It certainly doesn't seem so," she said. "Why, when the board heard what that architect's plan would cost—we wouldn't be able to buy a single new book for twenty years if we spent that much for a building."

"Then can't you look around for something a little bigger to rent?" said Mrs. Smith. "Even an empty store, maybe?"

"We've looked and looked," the librarian said, shaking her head again. "There just isn't a store available that has any more space than we have now. So I suppose we will simply have to make do."

"That is a shame," said Mrs. Smith. "This is so far out of town—and even if it wasn't, the traffic is so bad I just can't let Timothy walk, or even ride his bike."

"I know. I know." Miss Wickersham sighed again.

Timothy had seen Nan drift over to the corner where the picture books were. But he

[16]

stayed right beside the desk, waiting another chance.

"Please!" he now said. "I'd put everything back where I found it. I just need to have a telescope now!"

Timothy didn't really mean to fish for sympathy because of that taped wrist. But he couldn't help it, could he, if a little spot under the bandage had just started to itch furiously? So naturally he had to scratch it some. With a quick sideway glance, he saw Miss Wickersham's eyes soften.

"I'll tell you what," she said. "I'll let one of the seniors take over the desk here for a few moments, and I'll go down with you myself. I am quite sure there is a book about great men in science with a chapter on the man in Holland who made the first simple telescope. That should help you."

So down to the stacks went Timothy and Miss Wickersham.

[17]

Down to the grimy garage with all the trucks, then down a dark stone stairway to a damp and dusty basement packed with books, fat books, thin books, green books, blue books, stacks of books, books, books, with nobody to read them.

"Ugh!" Miss Wickersham said. "Dusty! Dirty!"

The single unshaded light bulb at the foot of the stairway was not much use as they threaded their way through narrow aisles between sagging plain wood shelves.

"Here we come now," Miss Wickersham said. "Astronomy. Oh, it is a shame, so many good books, such a waste."

"Doesn't anybody come down here?" Timothy asked.

"Not very often. We do try to discourage it. There's no room for brousing, and no light, and the stairway is so bad that we'd have people taking nasty falls all the time. But I suppose sooner or later we'll have to fix it up if

[18]

we're to stay here," she said in a discouraged tone.

"Yes'm," said Timothy, anxious now to take a look at a few of those books. He saw a tall blue one with silver stars and planets on the binding, a thin red one about a boy and his telescope, a gray one on just the moon.

Miss Wickersham drew out the thick brown one she'd had in mind, then stood, a smile glowing on her plump little face, as Timothy bent and picked one, two, three other books.

"Could I have them all?" he asked hesitantly.

"I don't see why not," said Miss Wickersham. "But, here, let me carry them. You're going to have to hold onto the railing with your good hand."

"Well!" said Mrs. Smith as they came back up the second flight of steps. "I see you found what you were looking for."

"Yup!" Timothy grinned. "That brown one has telescope diagrams. And one of the others, maps of the stars and things. Now all I need is a couple of pairs of old eyeglasses."

"Shhhhhhhh!" said Miss Wickersham, putting a finger to her lips. But she was still smiling.

"Come on, Nan," Mrs. Smith called softly. "We're ready now."

Trying to keep three books of all different sizes from slipping out of her hands, Nan stood up from her low bench and started for

the desk. One book slid down. Bending to pick it up, she dropped the others. Naturally she had to just stop and giggle.

"Here, let me help," said Mrs. Smith, taking the tallest, widest book.

"That's about a girl with geese," Nan said excitedly. "And this is a horse one, and a dog one. Say, Mom, can we stop at Purdy's Park on the way home. I really, really want to feed those ducks. We haven't for ages."

Mrs. Smith sighed, but she didn't seem too displeased.

"I suppose so," she said. "I'll drop you off, then I can stop for a head of lettuce down the street. What do you say, Timothy? Do you want to feed the ducks, too? Then I'll be able to go right on home, and you two can walk back when you're finished."

A little scowl had started, but Timothy shook it away. All right, the books would keep an hour or so, and any boy with a sister just going on seven knows you sometimes have to walk her home from someplace she can't walk home from by herself.

"Okay," said Timothy not too happily, but he said it.

"Good!" said Mrs. Smith.

# *Ducks and—*

THE pond in Purdy's Park was no more than a block or so from Main Street's stores. But once you ambled onto the gravel path that started at the high school corner, you were walking under great old oaks and maples that made it seem you'd found a forest.

By the time you got in as far as the pond, you couldn't even see Main Street if you tried, and the faint hum of cars sounded miles away in the distance.

"Look! Look!" Nan tapped excitedly on Timothy's arm.

There, near the low stone dam were dozens

of flipping, flapping soft gray mallard ducks. Little glints of sun from gaps in the tree leaves shone down on their green heads.

"Aren't they gorgeous?" Nan breathed.

Timothy had to admit that they looked pretty nice. "You want me to whistle?" he asked.

"Oh, no!" Nan shook her head fast several times. "You know that scared them last time. Then they wouldn't even come."

"They just didn't feel like eating that day," Timothy said patiently. "If they want to, they'll come all right, they're so tame. But if you don't call them, how are they supposed to know you have something to give them?"

With more than a slight amount of envy, he eyed the brown paper bag Nan clutched. In it were a couple of stale rolls from the bakery where they had just stopped with their mother.

If the duck-feeding had been his idea, then he would have had the bag of rolls. And

he could have whistled if he felt like it. But
this way . . .

"All right," he said a little grumpily. "You
feed your old ducks any way you want to.
But I'm not going to just stand around and
hope they're going to show up."

He turned and bent to pick up a twig
shaped like a fork. For no special reason, just
because it was there.

"You're not mad?" Nan asked.

[26]

"Nope." Timothy tried scratching his back with the twig. He really wasn't mad, merely a little grumpy. He'd much rather be home getting busy on the telescope project.

But Nan couldn't walk back by herself so here he was.

"Want a roll to crumble up?" Nan asked as she held out her bag.

"Nope," Timothy said. Of course he did

[27]

want one, but something would not let him say it. "You just go ahead. I'll be right around."

And he began to walk aimlessly down a side path under the trees.

By now Nan was breaking up one of her rolls, and she just nodded without looking around. Timothy kept going, kicking pebbles with his sneakered toes. Then, for no special reason at all, he stopped and said to himself: why not take a look at the old station? Not that he'd be likely to see much.

It was a station with no trains!

Well, not really no trains at all. Every morning before most people were awake, about a quarter to six, two musty passenger cars and an engine would lumber along. Then some time about half past seven in the evening, the same tired train would come by in the other direction.

That was all, except for, maybe once a month, a little string of dingy freight cars.

[28]

Well, did Timothy pick an afternoon when a freight was coming through? And did he save it from being wrecked, or something gory like that?

Not a bit.

Timothy met Mr. Drake.

 *Mr. Drake*

TIMOTHY walked cautiously across the shady little road that separated the back edge of the park from the station.

It wasn't that he had to watch out for cars —the little road that wandered in from Main Street led no place else except to the old station, so there weren't any cars.

It was just that, even in the middle of a warm, sunny August afternoon, the whole place had a strange, silent, slightly spooky look about it.

Thick ivy vines had grown up over the years to almost cover the gray stone of the station building. Not small by any means, it was big enough to be somebody's house, with a sort of porch in the front which you could imagine a horse and buggy trotting up to. Then, on either side patches of tree-shaded grass sloped down to an old wooden plat-form along the tracks.

Timothy stepped into the shadows under the roof of the little porch. And then he stopped. Not that he was scared. Not exactly.

But he had heard something. Something that sounded like shuffling steps on the other side of the big wooden door into the station.

In a flash he thought back to the few other times he had come to take a look. Then he had been with a couple of other boys. And, now he remembered, they had just jumped around a little on the sagging planks of the platform beside the tracks. And never even gone into the station itself.

Maybe he shouldn't be staying around here. Nan might be finished with her duck feeding, and be looking for him.

Then suddenly—

THE DOOR OPENED ITSELF!

Timothy's heart gave a monstrous thump, and he turned to race back across that little road.

But he hadn't taken more than a step when he heard a queer, scratchy voice call out: "You don't have to run, young fellow."

Timothy turned, and he saw a tiny, twinkly-eyed old man with a fluff of white, white hair and the biggest whitest mustache you can possibly picture. He was wearing a rumpled gray uniform, and he was smiling.

"Guess I gave you a right good scare," the old man said, still smiling. "Didn't mean to do that, but, now, let's get a look at you."

Putting a serious expression on his wrinkly face, he pulled at one piece of his mustache and stared hard at Timothy for a few seconds. Then the smile came back.

"You look all right," the old man said.

"Not the type to go carving your name on somebody's wall, I'd say."

He stopped as if he were waiting for an answer. Timothy's eyes were about popping at the oddness of it all, but he still managed to say: "Oh, no, sir!"

"You'd never believe it," the old man said, stroking a piece of that mustache again, "you'd never believe it the way some young scamps would cut right into Mr. Purdy's walnut walls that he had sent all the way from England."

Now Timothy just couldn't hold in his astonishment.

"Walnut walls?" His voice came out squeaky. "Sent from England?"

"Just step inside with me and I'll show you," the old man said. "You might think this is just like any railroad station, young fellow, but the truth of it is that it's absolutely the only one of its kind in the whole United States."

[34]

The truth of it was that Timothy was already quite convinced this wasn't like any other railroad station. Not like the bustly one over near the river, where you had to stand in line to buy a ticket to the city. Nor like the tremendous one in the city.

Anybody could see this station wasn't a busy place, like all the others he knew about. But what could be so special about the inside of it?

Stepping into a large, dim room with a ceiling as high as two ordinary rooms put one on top of the other, Timothy still couldn't see what the man was talking about.

"Well, now, take a good look at that walnut paneling," the little old man said, pointing at the glossy dark wood lining the walls. "Mr. Purdy had that brought, every stick of it, from a duke's house near the English town where he was born."

"Oh!" What else could Timothy say?

"Yes, indeedy," the old man went on,

drawing a pipe with a curved stem out of a pocket of his rumpled jacket.

"When Matthew J. Purdy did something, young fellow, he did it right. Why, do you know that in the old days the floor"—Timothy hastily glanced down at the smooth stone squares underfoot—"was covered by the finest carpet in the land. Oh, the rich reds and greens in it! Yes, sir, the finest rug from Persia was none too good for Mr. Purdy's station!"

The old man gave a little shake of his white head. Then he motioned for Timothy to sit beside him on the dark wooden bench along the wall.

His head filled with questions, Timothy sat down. Did this use to be Mr. Purdy's house? And the park, his farm or something?

But the old man didn't wait to be asked.

"Mr. Purdy was a poor man when he first came to this country," he said, and he puffed a second on his unlit pipe. "Did you know

[36]

that? A poor weaver of cloth, he was, but smart as a whip. It wasn't long before he had a small mill of his own, and then another. And then he came up here and moved his family into the grandest mansion anybody in these parts had ever seen."

The old man sighed and gave a sad little tug at a piece of his mustache.

"I was a mere boy then, helping around the garden," he said. "It wasn't till some years later that Mr. Purdy got the railroad to let him build this station. By then I was old enough to have the job as agent.

"Then Mr. Purdy would come around and say to me, Mr. Drake, he would say, Mr. Drake, do you realize you are working in a veritable palace?"

Timothy was biting the tip of one thumb. Then this was Mr. Drake, the station agent, he thought.

"Oh, it wasn't easy for Mr. Purdy to convince the railroad to move away the old station that used to be here, forty, fifty years ago," Mr. Drake said.

"They had no trucks and bulldozers and suchlike in those days, you know. But they did need a freight station over by Mill Creek, and finally Mr. Purdy persuaded them to hoist the old shack here up onto a platform and have horses tow the whole thing a couple of miles down the pike.

"No doubt Mr. Purdy did pay the bill for all this, but he was bound and determined to have a nice place for his guests to arrive at. No automobiles in those days, young fellow, least ways none that could zoom up from the city in just an hour or so. To come out here, you had to take a train."

Mr. Drake chewed on his unlit pipe for a few seconds, then took it out of his mouth again.

Timothy was watching wide-eyed.

[39]

"And those trains!" the old man said, rubbing a hand through his thick white hair. "They were just building the new tracks over by the river then, so every train to and from the city would come by here. They wouldn't all stop, of course. Even so, you got to hear a good, long, too-ooo-ooot! too-ooo-ooot! from a real engine couple of times a day."

"Steam engines?" Timothy said, suddenly forgetting whatever other questions he'd wanted to ask.

"Yes, indeedy, steam engines," Mr. Drake said. "Big black engines, black as the coal they burned, not like the ladylike ones you see these days. But I suppose Mr. Sylvester P. King just doesn't care for steam engines. Mr. Sylvester P. King doesn't care for railroads at all, far as I can make out. But, mind, I'm not going to grumble. I know the world has changed." And he gave a sad little bob of his white head.

[40]

"Mr. Drake, who is—" Timothy started to say.

"Mr. Sylvester P. King is the president of the railroad," Mr. Drake said. "In charge of the whole works." He shook his head again.

"Wrote me a letter telling me I ought to quit as agent here," Mr. Drake said bitterly. Then he shrugged his thin shoulders.

"Course, that was after the branch superintendent tried it first. But I just wrote right back to Mr. Sylvester P. King and I told him as long as there's a station here I'm going to be agent, and that's final."

Mr. Drake suddenly gave a short, cackling laugh.

"Bet he's not used to being talked to that way," the old man said. "But I have to say he was decent about it. Wrote back I could stay on 'pending a decision on the future of the station,' whatever that means.

"Whatever it means, I'm staying. Even if it is a lonesome sort of job these days. Would you believe it, for the whole of last month I took in exactly $4.02? Four dollars and two cents. Not like in the old days, I can tell you.

"Poor Mr. Purdy!" said Mr. Drake. "Course he passed on twenty, thirty years ago, but he wouldn't like it a bit to know what's happened to his station.

"Now the park he gave the town—that's another story. It was just a couple of acres of raggedy woods when he bought it and gave it to the town just after the old high school was built across the way. Not the school that's

there now, but the one before it. Anyway, that's a fine park now, and he would like it.

"And as for his own mansion house out Somertown Road, I don't think he'd mind at all to see it a research center, or whatever you call it. The station, though! Such a waste . . ."

"But those steam engines—" Timothy said.

"Steam engines?" Mr. Drake looked puzzled. Then his smile shone again and he nodded. "Steam engines! Young fellow, I can tell you—"

Into the cool, dim room came a faint cry: "Tim-o-thy! Oh, Tim-o-thy!"

Timothy jumped up from the bench.

"Gosh! Nan!" he said. "I have to go now, Mr. Drake."

The old man smiled.

"It's been a real pleasure talking with you," he said. "Come back sometime, young fellow. I think I have some photographs of a few of the old engines tucked away in a drawer in there." He pointed toward an open

[43]

door in the far corner of the room which led
into his small office.

Timothy nodded.

"I'll be back!" he promised.

 # "Do It!"

I T WAS after supper and the shadows on
the lawn showed that Nan's day was almost over. Sitting curled in one corner of the
porch glider, she said: "Timothy!"

Bent over one of his new library books, he
didn't even seem to have heard her.

"Timothy!" She tried again, a little louder.

Still no answer, so this time she shouted:
"TIMOTHY!"

The light was getting a bit too dim to read
by, so Timothy put down his book and said:
"Want to catch some fireflies?"

Nan shook her head. Now it happened

this was just exactly what she'd had in mind when she tried to make him look up from his book. But anybody knows a girl has to change her mind sometimes.

"Did he really, really say there used to be a rug on the floor in that station?" she asked, for she had been thinking over the station story before the fireflies idea came up.

"Sure he did," Timothy said. If you lived in the same house with Nan, you would have been just as used to unexpected questions as Timothy was.

"It's a real shame nobody ever goes there now," Nan murmured. "Poor Mr. Drake must get awfully lonesome."

Timothy gave a little shrug.

"If they'd just get some good old steam engines back, or even some regular trains, he'd have plenty of company."

"The railroad ought to do that," Nan said. "I mean, have some more trains go by. It's

[46]

such a nice station. Say, maybe we could get Dad to ask them to send some more trains out."

Timothy just shook his head and gave her that girls-are-silly look.

"Then maybe we could ask the railroad ourselves," Nan insisted. "I mean, maybe they've just forgot all about having such a nice station here. You said Mr. Drake wrote a letter to the president of the railroad. You can write letters. I know you can. Why don't you write to him, too?"

Timothy shook his head harder.

"That's—" he started. But any boy knows some things are just no use, so he stopped.

"Why not?" Nan demanded.

Timothy sighed an immense sigh and then he said: "Because they have a perfectly good station just a couple of miles away and it's on the main line that goes right down to the city. And even if there were more trains right here,

[47]

hardly anybody would ever take them, because you have to change. Anybody knows
that.

"What they really ought to do is close down
the whole branch line," Timothy continued,
"and then they could let you use the station
to play house in, or something."

But Nan refused to get insulted.

"They wouldn't do that," she said. "But
since it's such a fancy place, maybe somebody
who doesn't have a nice house now could
move in and live there."

"A duke or something?" Timothy said, and
he gave the glider a hard push. "You know a
duke or perhaps a prince or princess looking
for a house? Mr. Drake called it a palace."

Nan lifted her light brown eyebrows till
they almost touched her bangs.

"I'll bet there are plenty of people who'd
like a house so near the high school and all the
stores," she said, "and near a park with ducks.
And you could fix it up a little, put in some
[48]

walls and things if you didn't want such a great big room and—"

Great big room! Right near the high school and all the stores!

Timothy was thinking something in the back of his mind, and suddenly he jumped right up from the glider.

"The library!" he shouted. "It could be a station-library! Wow, what an idea!"

Nan was studying her brother with a look

of absolute, adoring astonishment on her own small, round face.

"That's right!" she whispered. "Oh, let's call Miss What's-her-name right this minute."

Timothy shook his head.

"Nope," he said. "I'm going to do what you said before. I'm going to write a letter. To the president of the railroad."

Nan's pony tails gave a most furious bounce.

"Do it!" she said. "Oh, Timothy, let's do it! Do it! Do it!"

The Letter

WITH Nan trailing a step or two behind him, Timothy crossed that little road from the park to the station about half past nine the next morning and hurried up to the front door. Even before he had opened it, he was calling: "Mr. Drake! Say, Mr. Drake!"

Shuffling out of his small office in the far corner of the big, dim room, Mr. Drake stopped when he saw them and smiled delightedly.

"Well, young fellow!" he said. "Didn't expect to see you again so soon. And the little girl, too. Come in, come in."

"We wanted—" Timothy began.

"Now don't tell me," the old man said. "What is it could draw two young ones in on such a fine, sunny morning? It's those steam engines, I know it!"

"But—" Timothy said.

"Now I'm going to empty out that drawer right this instant to see if I can't find the photographs," Mr. Drake said. "It may take time, I warn you. A lot of things accumulate in more than forty years. But you just come with me, and I'll give you some old timetables to look at meanwhile."

"But Mr. Drake—" Timothy tried again.

"Maybe you'd rather look at my telegraph code book," the old man said. "Not much use in it these days, but you could learn the dots and dashes.

"And, young lady, what say you take a turn

with some of my housecleaning chores? I have a real, old-fashioned feather duster inside. Bet you've never seen the likes of it. Have to keep the dust from gathering on Mr. Purdy's walls even if—"

"But, Mr. Drake!" Nan said. It wasn't that she said it in such a loud voice—as much as the way she said it. Even Mr. Drake just had to listen.

"Mr. Drake, we have something to show you first," she said.

"Right here," Timothy popped in, ready to take advantage of her opening. He hastily reached into a pocket of his jeans and held out a folded sheet of paper.

"It's a letter," Nan said. "Timothy wrote it. But you have to help us because we don't know where to send it."

Mr. Drake was looking from one excited young face to the other, and his own face was extra wrinkly as if he was a little worried.

"Now what have you two been up to?" he

asked. "It's not something that's going to make trouble, is it?"

"Oh, no!" Nan said.

Timothy shook his head fast. "It should help you," he said. "At least I think so."

"So the station won't be so lonesome anymore," Nan said.

"See, the library is in an awful dinky, dirty old building," Timothy said almost at the same time.

"Whoa, there!" said Mr. Drake with a tug at his white mustache. "One at a time now. All right, young fellow, what's this all about?"

"Well, I fell out of my tree house yesterday," Timothy said with a glance at his bandaged wrist, "and then we decided to build a telescope and so we had to go to the library—"

"Mom had to drive us, it's so far away," Nan put in. "But we'll be able to walk here by ourselves, at least Timothy can, and when I'm eight I'll be able to, too."

[56]

Timothy flashed her a look that said please-be-still-a-minute, then he went on: "Well, anyway, the library had to move out of the Village Hall when the police needed more room, and the only place they could find was on top of the truck garage, and there's no room there except in a dirty old cellar for lots of the books on telescopes and things—"

"Oh-ho!" said Mr. Drake, starting to nod his white head. "So you think maybe the library could move in here?" From his face you could see he wasn't too sure what to think about this yet.

"But you wouldn't have to move," Nan said earnestly. "I mean, you could still have your little office, and anyone who wanted to could come in and visit after they got their books. We would."

"Sure, and you could look at all the books and magazines," Timothy said. "Miss Wickersham wouldn't mind and—"

"Is this Miss Wickersham in charge of the

[57]

library?" Mr. Drake asked. At their nod, he added: "You been around to talk to her about this yet?"

"Well, no," said Timothy. "I thought we should write this letter first to the same man you wrote to—the president of the railroad.

"If he says yes, we can ask her. She ought to be in favor of the idea. She said yesterday they'd move to an empty store or anywhere to have more space, and this is much nicer than any old store."

Mr. Drake pulled thoughtfully at one piece of his mustache, and then he said: "It's been my experience, young fellow, that you never can tell what a lady's likely to think. But let's see that letter of yours."

This is what Timothy handed over:

Dear Sir,

You have a very nice Station in our town that nobody goes to because trains hardly ever come so we want to know if you would mind if the Library moved in. The Library really needs some place to move to because where they are now they have to keep lots of books in a dirty cellar. We hope you say yes.

Timothy and Nan Smith

P.S. Mr. Drake could still keep his office and let the books be just in the big room. That's much bigger than where the Library is now. Thanks a lot.

. . .

Mr. Drake took off the spectacles he had put on to read the letter, and he smiled.

"That's a fine letter you wrote, young fellow," he said. "I can't see where it could do any harm. But, mind, don't be too hopeful it'll do any good. Mr. Sylvester P. King just might not like the idea. But send it, go ahead. Here's what you write on the envelope."

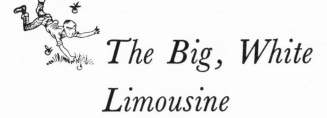

The Big, White Limousine

"DID the mail come yet?" Timothy called in from the porch.

Mrs. Smith shook her head and sighed.

"Timothy," she said, "have you been sending away for things again?" Shredded glass that was supposed to be stuffed inside the walls of houses was still clinging to his rug from the last batch of free samples.

But Timothy didn't have to answer, for just then Nan bounded down the steps and said: "Mom, has the mailman come by?"

"You, too?" said Mrs. Smith. "Now what on earth have the both of you been up to?"

Nan's blue eyes widened innocently.

"Nothing," she said. "I mean, I guess two days is too soon to get an answer." And she turned to start back up the steps to her room where she was dressing dolls.

"Wait one minute, young lady," Mrs. Smith said. "I want to hear what's going on, so—"

She stopped at the unmistakable sound of a car door slamming right outside in their driveway.

"Who could that be?" she said.

Just that second Timothy rushed in from the porch.

"Wow!" he shouted. "You should see it. A huge, white limo-limo—"

Mrs. Smith hurried out to take a look.

"Limousine," she said over her shoulder. She seemed more than a trifle astonished at the size and the color of the car. Two strange men who had obviously just gotten out of

[62]

it were walking right up to the screen door.

"Mrs. Smith?" the first man said, smiling. "And this must be Timothy—and Nan."

"Why, yes," said Mrs. Smith. "But who—"

The first man, a little bit taller, broader, and bossier than the other, took a small white card out of his wallet and handed it to her.

"Jonathan J. Weaver, assistant to the president," Mrs. Smith read aloud in a puzzled voice. "President of what? Oh, I see, the railroad. But—"

"The railroad!" said Timothy.

"Ooooooooooooh!" said Nan.

"And this," said Mr. Weaver, nodding to the shorter, thinner man beside him, "this is Mr. Mole, our director of community relations."

"How do you do?" said Mrs. Smith. "Please come in. But, could you tell me . . ."

"You see!" Mr. Mole said, tapping Mr. Weaver on the arm. "Doesn't know a thing about it. I thought so. They did it all by themselves. I told S. P. it was genuine!"

Mrs. Smith sank down on the glider.

"What is it they did all by themselves?" she said. Then hastily: "But whatever it was, I'm sure they meant well. They're good children and—"

"Now, now, Mrs. Smith," said Mr. Weaver. "Calm yourself. They haven't done anything wrong."

"Righto!" said Mr. Mole.

"You should be proud of them," Mr. Weaver said. "As the father of four myself, I assure you you'll be proud."

"But what—" Mrs. Smith began again.

Mr. Weaver reached into his wallet again and took out a folded sheet of paper which looked very familiar to Timothy and Nan.

Huddling together near the door, utterly speechless at the turn things had taken, they watched their mother unfold the letter and read it.

[64]

"What-a-a-a-t?" said Mrs. Smith after a quick glance at it. Then, in a more normal voice: "Timothy, did you write this?"

Timothy gulped.

"Why, sure, Mom," he said. "It says my name, doesn't it?"

A smile broke through onto her face.

"It certainly does," she said. "But what made you write it? Wherever did you get the idea?"

"It was Nan's idea to write a letter," Timothy said.

"But it was his idea about the library moving to the station," Nan put in softly.

Mrs. Smith was shaking her head slowly from side to side.

"Why nobody else ever thought of it . . . ?" she murmured, and shook her head some more.

"It does sound, ah, interesting," said Mr. Weaver. "Our president, Mr. King, asked us to come up and investigate. To see if such an unusual idea could really work out."

"Like to do you folks a good turn if we can," Mr. Mole said.

"Now, we're not promising anything," Mr. Weaver said. "But Mr. King wants us to give him a report after we take a look at the station and the library. He has a notion this station is a good, solid building put up in the old days by a rich man in these parts who wanted his guests to arrive at the fanciest depot on the line."

"Mr. Purdy," Timothy offered in a small voice.

"Purdy?" said Mr. Mole. "Could be. S. P. said it was something like 'birdie.' Nothing on it in the files, though."

"In any case," Mr. Weaver said, "we expect to be shutting down all service on this branch line one of these days. If the station is really big enough, perhaps it could be part station, part library for the time being, and eventually all library. But as I said, we're not promising anything. We'll have to see."

Mrs. Smith was rubbing her forehead in astonishment.

"Who would have thought it?" she murmured.

Nan beamed at her brother.

"He thought it!" she said.

"Aw!" said Timothy, the way a brother had to.

[68]

"Well, then," said Mr. Weaver, rising. "With your permission, Mrs. Smith, we'd like Timothy and Nan to come along with us to the library and the station. To show us around, be our guides, you might say. We'll have them home by lunchtime."

"Ride in that?" Timothy's voice came out squeaky with awe as he pointed to the big white car.

Mr. Weaver smiled.

"As the father of four myself, I thought you might not mind a ride in Mr. King's limousine," he said. "Come, let's get started. We have a lot of inspecting to do."

Oompah! Oompah!

TIMOTHY scowled as he ran a comb through his short reddish hair.

Of all the silly things, to have to get dressed up on a Saturday morning! Especially the last Saturday morning before another whole year of school. Just to go shopping!

Not that it would be so bad going back to school. Nothing much interesting seemed to be happening the last few weeks, not even anything about the station-library business. And for some reason there was a new rule the last two weeks or so about not even walking over to the park or the station. Timothy shook his head. Everybody knew mothers sometimes would get silly ideas, but this one was the silliest!

Except maybe the idea about getting all scrubbed and rubbed just to go shopping this morning. Actually, he did need a couple of pairs of new slacks because last year's hardly came past his knees, but why make such a fuss about it?

"Timothy!" That was Mom, trying to hurry him.

"Okay. Coming."

Down in the hall Nan was standing nice and still while her pony tails got a good, stiff brushing. But you can't expect a girl to mind that sort of thing when it's going to lead to a whole batch of new skirts.

"All set," said Mrs. Smith, putting down the brush. "Come on, Dan!" she called in to Mr. Smith.

Slipping his arms into the sleeves of a regular, week-day, going-to-work suit jacket,

Mr. Smith strolled in from the porch and said: "Ready?"

"What goes on here?" Timothy said. It was confusing for Dad to be serious about coming along. "You're not really coming SHOPPING, are you?"

"And why not?" said Mr. Smith. "If I'm going to pay the bills, I might as well see the money go, for once."

Timothy shook his head. Something fishy was going on, Dad in a suit jacket on Saturday morning, coming to watch them try on clothes. Then he shrugged. If they weren't going to say anything, he'd just have to wait and see.

In the car it was Nan who noticed first.

"Dad!" she said. "You forgot to turn on Maple Street. You have to, to get into the parking-lot in back of the stores."

"Never mind, young lady," said Mr. Smith cheerfully. And then, driving right on past the last of the stores on Main Street, he drove into the little winding road that led—to the old railroad station.

"Hey!" said Timothy. "Where are we going? And look at that. Cars parked all along here."

Sure enough, there were cars, bumper to bumper, parked all along one side of the narrow road, barely leaving room for Mr. Smith to squeeze on toward the station.

And there was Big Tom, the school policeman, waving for them to take an empty space right smack across from the station itself.

And the station!

Red, white, and blue banners were draped over the little porch, where a mob of people was standing.

Two shiny blue ribbons were hung between the pillars on either side of the front door.

And there, beside the door, a new brass sign had been attached. On it big, gleaming letters said: TOWN LIBRARY.

"Timothy!" Nan said breathlessly. "Look! Just look! Does it say 'Library?' I bet it does!"

"It does," Timothy said in a dazed voice. Very slowly he shook his head three times.

"I hope you don't mind if we go shopping after lunch," Mrs. Smith said.

"Let's go!" said Mr. Smith. "I hear there's a parade coming by pretty soon."

As they climbed out of the car, people in the crowd beside the station started to wave as if they'd been waiting just for the Smiths.

There was Miss Wickersham, and Mr. Drake. Schoolteachers, the man from the bank. All smiling away.

"Timothy." Nan nudged her brother. "Do you think they all know we sort of started this?"

"Don't be silly," Timothy whispered. But something somewhere way inside of him was asking the same question. And if they did all know, my gosh, it might be like a school

[74]

assembly where you had to stand up and . . .

"Chin up!" said Mr. Smith. "You're going to have some fun."

Just then, even above the sounds close by them, came the deep, booming Oompah! Oompah! of a band off in the distance.

"Parade's coming!" Mrs. Smith said. "Come on, let's cross so we won't be in the way."

First came the band, with the players in their crimson suits with the shiny gold stripes. Then came the Girl Scouts and the Boy Scouts and just about everybody in town who wasn't there already.

Timothy and Nan stood numbly by their parents' side.

Then Mayor Tweedy raised his hand for quiet. "Folks!" he said. "We're here to open up absolutely the most unusual library in the whole length and breadth of the land."

Clapping started then, but Mayor Tweedy raised his hand for silence again.

[75]

"You'll see when the ribbons are cut that it's a beauty!" he shouted. "We just built a balcony over most of the big room inside, with good strong stairs leading right up to it. Now we have two stories of books.

"What's more, the old baggage room will be a study room right next to Mr. Drake's little office, where you can still drop in and see him. And in nice weather you can sit and

read your books on our trackside reading-terrace and maybe even see a train go by once in awhile!"

Mayor Tweedy paused for the laugh that rippled through the crowd, then, smiling, said: "I want to thank all the railroad people for making this possible. And for helping to get the balcony built and the books moved so fast."

Applause broke out again.

By his father's side Timothy suddenly frowned.

"That's funny!' he said. "I don't see Mr. Weaver and Mr. Mole."

Mr. Smith smiled a smile that said I-know-something-you-don't-know. "Just you wait," he whispered.

Mayor Tweedy raised his hand again.

"I also want to thank Miss Wickersham," he said. "She worked till midnight every night this week arranging books!"

More applause, and Miss Wickersham's plump face flushed pink with pleasure. Then the Mayor went on: "But most of all I want to thank—Timothy and Nan Smith!"

And then the cheering started.

Oh-oh, Timothy thought. It might sound crazy, but he turned pale, then pink, and scared, then pleased, all in a couple of seconds.

As for Nan, she clutched tight to her

[78]

mother's hand and looked the way a girl would look if, well if she'd just been picked to make the first trip in a rocket ship to Mars.

Above all the noise the Mayor shouted: "Come on up here, kids, and let us all say thanks for thinking this up."

Like a dream, Timothy and Nan stepped forward.

The cheering started again, and rose and rose. But suddenly another sound rose above it.

Too-ooo-ooot! Too-ooo-ooot! Too-ooo-ooot!

Could it be? It was! A real, old-fashioned steam engine was coming tooting down the tracks.

"All right, folks!" Mayor Tweedy shouted. "Here they come now, right on schedule!"

The band started playing again, and everybody clapped and stamped and danced around. A little old coal black engine draw-

[79]

ing one small wooden car jolted to a stop right beside the station.

The engineer waved and tooted his whistle.

Then down the steps of the old wooden car walked Mr. Weaver and Mr. Mole and a tremendous mountain of a man who had to be Mr. Sylvester P. King.

"So that's the boy!" boomed Mr. Sylvester P. King.

Timothy gulped. And gulped again. And rubbed a hand across his eyes as if he just couldn't trust what he was seeing.

As for Nan, she clutched at Timothy's arm and stared the most astonished stare you ever saw.

"Welcome! Welcome!" Mayor Tweedy was shouting. "Now I guess we can get on with the ribbon-cutting. Where's the scissors? Oh, here! All right, Nan, let's see you snip."

"Go on," Timothy whispered.

[80]

Nan stepped up and took the long silver scissors the Mayor was holding out.

"Th-that ribbon?" she said.

Mayor Tweedy nodded.

Snip! And the crowd shouted some more.

"Fine, fine," said Mr. Weaver.

"Good girl!" boomed Mr. Sylvester P. King.

Nan's face suddenly crinkled into the biggest, brightest smile you ever saw, and then her lips started to move slowly.

"Wow!" she said.

The crowd laughed and clapped, then quieted as Timothy took the scissors. You would have thought that pair of silver scissors was awfully hot the way he held them.

"Go on, boy!" boomed Mr. Sylvester P. King. "Don't want to keep that engineer waiting too long."

It took a few seconds for the words to sink in.

"You mean . . ." Timothy said. Then shook

[81]

his head. Of course, it couldn't be. It was just that the president of the railroad was in a hurry to get back to work.

But Mr. Sylvester P. King was nodding his huge head as if . . .

Snip! The second shiny blue ribbon was cut.

"All right, folks!" Mayor Tweedy shouted.

"Now you can come in and look around. The station-library is open! Step up, everybody."

The band struck up, and everybody cheered some more. Mr. Sylvester P. King stretched out one of his tremendous hands and grasped Timothy by the shoulder.

"This way, boy!" he boomed.

With his other great big hand, he took Nan's hand and said: "You, too, Miss!"

Too-ooo-ooot! Too-ooo-ooot! went the little engine.

"Had an idea you two might not mind a ride in the engine cab down to Mill Creek and back," Mr. Sylvester P. King hollered as he steered them toward the tracks.

"Mind?" Timothy's voice quavered.

As for Nan, that smile showed she positively wouldn't mind, either.

"Guess I had a pretty good idea," Mr. Sylvester P. King boomed in a satisfied voice. "But you had a pretty good idea, too. Now tell me. How'd you come to think of this library business?"

Timothy drew in a deep, deep breath. Then he said: "Well, you see, first I fell out of my tree house and . . ."

But now you know what happened all because of the wonderful tumble of Timothy Smith.

[84]

A NOTE ON THE AUTHOR

DORIS FABER, since her marriage and consequent retirement from the *New York Times* as a reporter, has contributed several suburban feature stories to that newspaper. The idea for *The Wonderful Tumble of Timothy Smith* came out of one of these articles. Mrs. Faber was brought up on Long Island and graduated from New York University. She now lives in Pleasantville, New York, with her husband and two daughters, Alice and Marjorie. This is Mrs. Faber's second book for young readers. Her first one, *Elaine Stinson, Campus Reporter* was published in 1955.

THE TEXT of this book has been set on the Linotype in Baskerville, a recutting of a type face originally designed by John Baskerville (1706-1775). Baskerville, who was a writing master in Birmingham, England, began experimenting about 1750 with type design and punch cutting. His first book, set throughout in his new types, was a Virgil in royal quarto, published in 1757. This was followed by his famous editions of Milton, the Bible, the Book of Common Prayer, and several Latin classic authors. His types, which are distinctive and elegant in design, were a forerunner of what we know today as the "modern" group of type faces. After his death, Baskerville's widow sold all his punches and matrices to the Société Philosophique, Littéraire et Typographique (totally embodied in the person of Beaumarchais, author of *The Barber of Seville* and *The Marriage of Figaro*), which used some of the types to print the seventy-volume edition, at Kehl, of Voltaire's works. After a checkered career in France, where they dropped out of sight for some years, the punches and matrices finally came into the possession of the distinguished Paris type-founders, Deberney & Peignot, who, in singularly generous fashion, presented them to the Cambridge University Press in 1953.